THE RAVEN

Adapted by
Joeming W. Dunn & Ashley Dunn

Illustrated by
Rod Espinosa

Based upon the works of
Edgar Allan Poe

magic
Wagon

visit us at
www.abdopublishing.com

Published by Magic Wagon, a division of the ABDO Group, PO Box 398166, Minneapolis, MN 55439. Copyright © 2014 by Abdo Consulting Group, Inc. International copyrights reserved in all countries. All rights reserved. No part of this book may be reproduced in any form without written permission from the publisher.

Graphic Planet™ is a trademark and logo of Magic Wagon.

Printed in the United States of America, North Mankato, Minnesota.
102013
012014
♻ This book contains at least 10% recycled materials.

Original story by Edgar Allan Poe
Adapted by Joeming Dunn
Illustrated by Rod Espinosa
Colored and lettered by Rod Espinosa
Edited by Stephanie Hedlund and Rochelle Baltzer
Interior layout and design by Antarctic Press
Cover art by Rod Espinosa
Cover design by Neil Klinepier

Library of Congress Cataloging-in-Publication Data

Dunn, Joeming W., author, adapter.
  The raven / adapted by Joeming Dunn ; illustrated by Rod Espinosa.
    pages cm. -- (Graphic horror)
  "Based upon the works of Edgar Allan Poe."
  Summary: Retells Edgar Allan Poe's classic horror poem The Raven in graphic novel form.
  ISBN 978-1-62402-017-9
1. Poe, Edgar Allan, 1809-1849. Raven--Adaptations. 2. Horror tales. 3. Graphic novels. [1. Graphic novels. 2. Horror stories. 3. Poe, Edgar Allan, 1809-1849. Raven--Adaptations.] I. Espinosa, Rod, illustrator. II. Title.
  PZ7.7.D86Rav 2014
  741.5'973--dc23
                    2013025320

TABLE OF CONTENTS

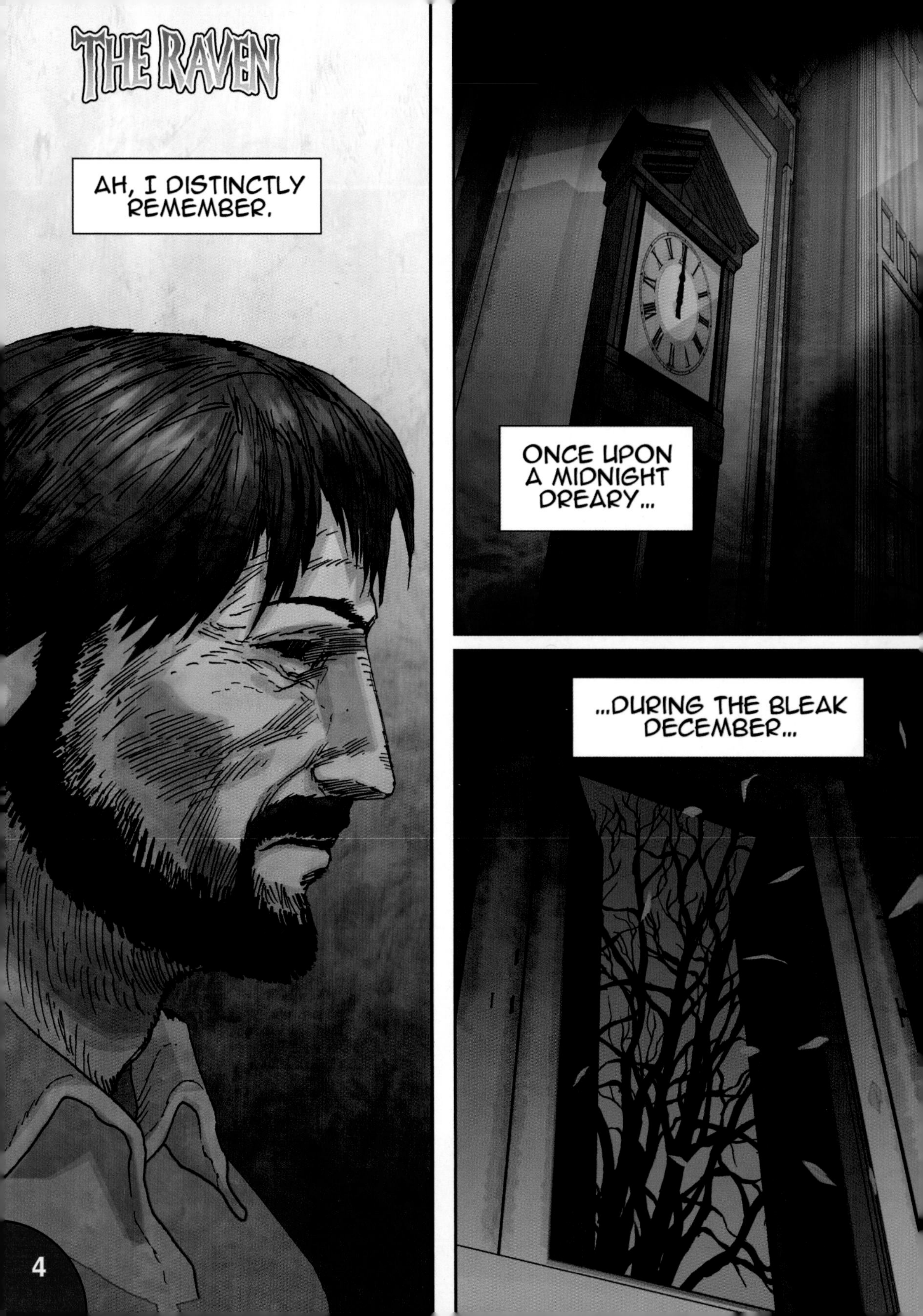
THE RAVEN
AH, I DISTINCTLY REMEMBER.
ONCE UPON A MIDNIGHT DREARY...
...DURING THE BLEAK DECEMBER...

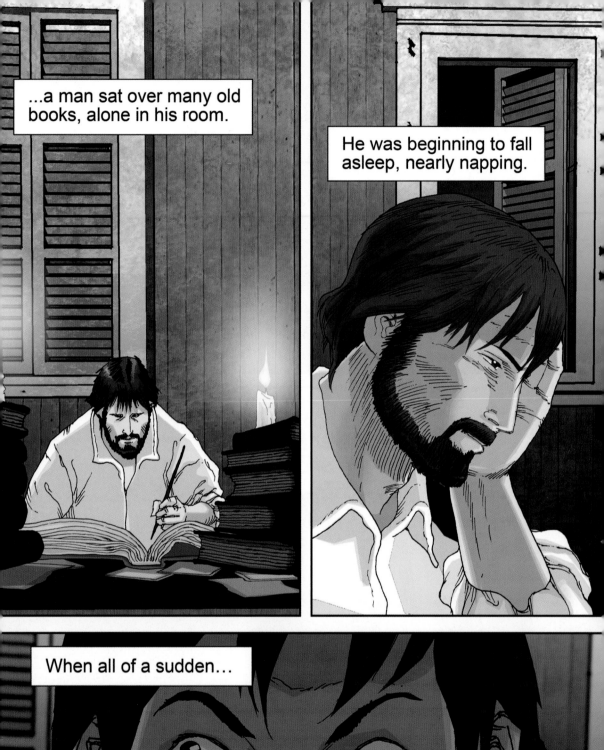

...a man sat over many old books, alone in his room.

He was beginning to fall asleep, nearly napping.

When all of a sudden…

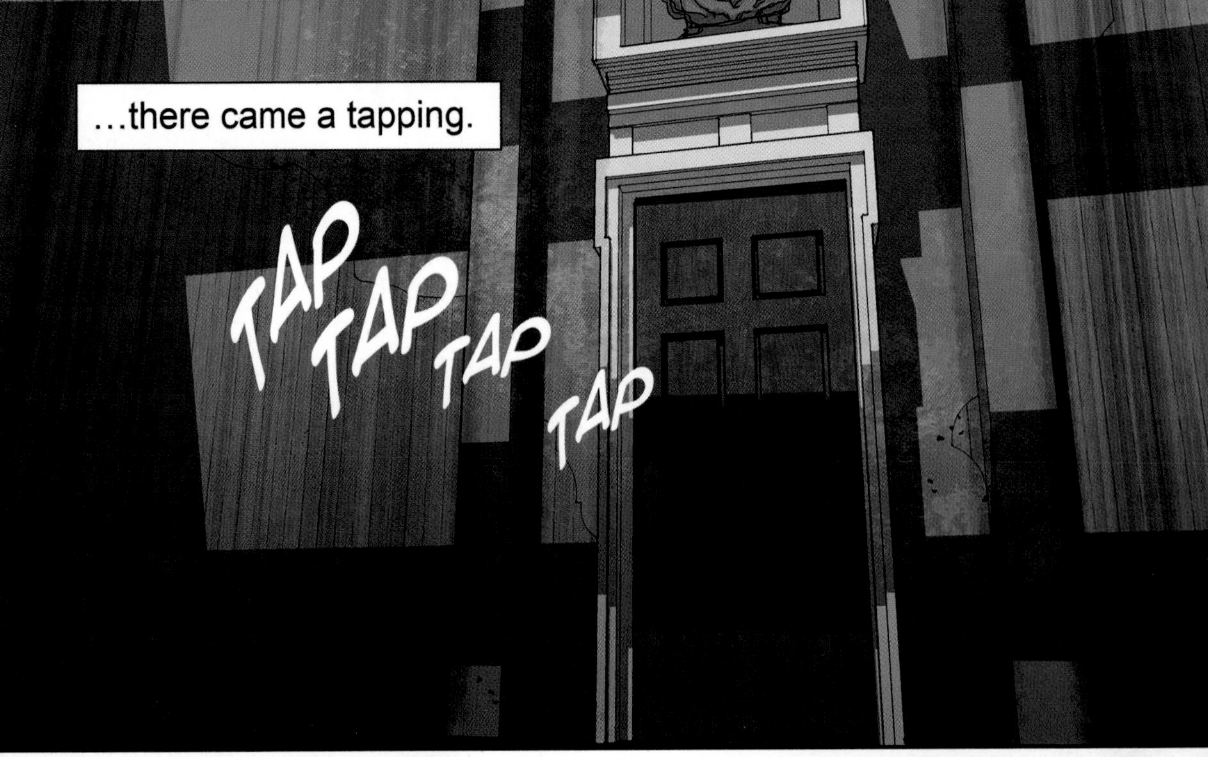
…there came a tapping.
TAP TAP TAP TAP

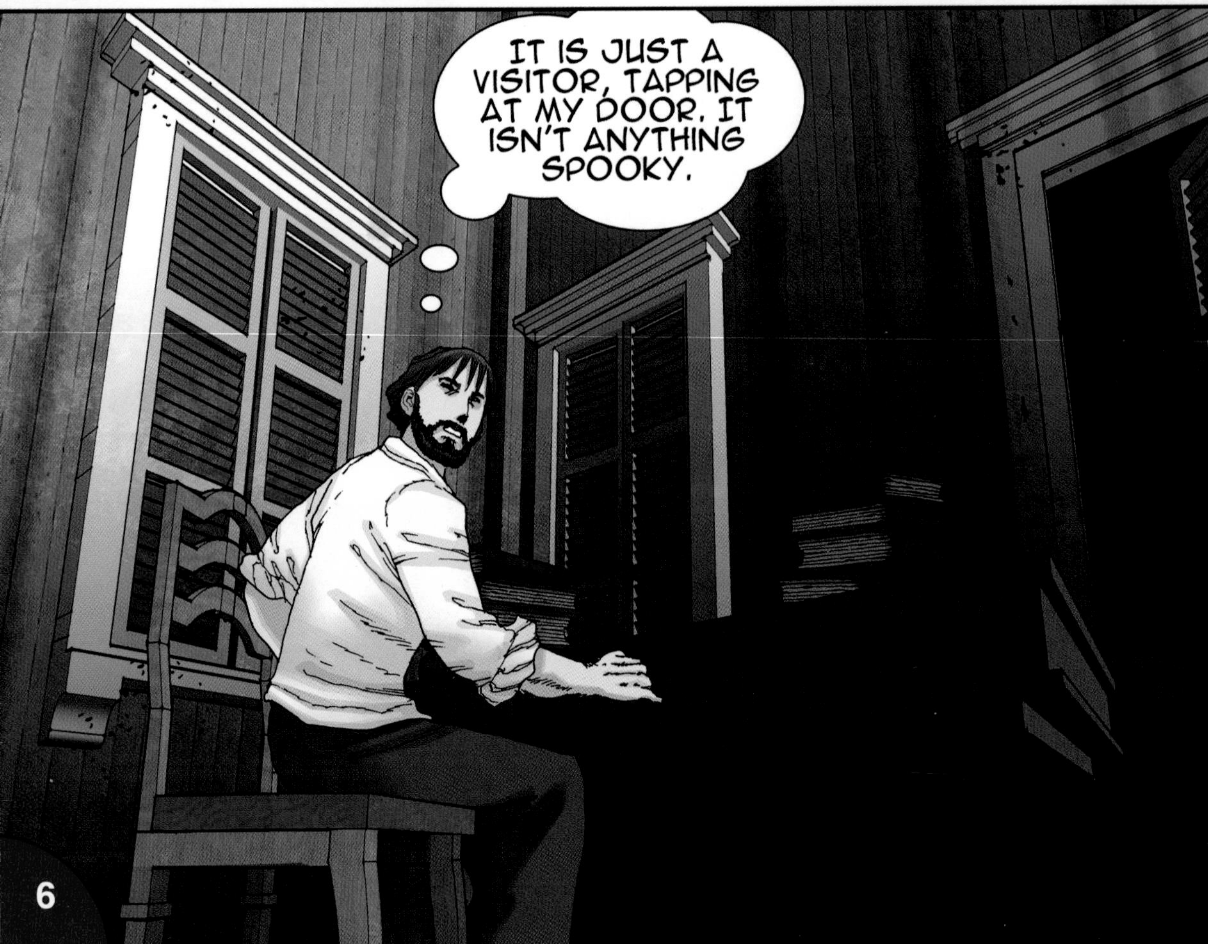
IT IS JUST A VISITOR, TAPPING AT MY DOOR. IT ISN'T ANYTHING SPOOKY.

The fire didn't help the mood. Each dying ember made ghostlike figures upon the floor.

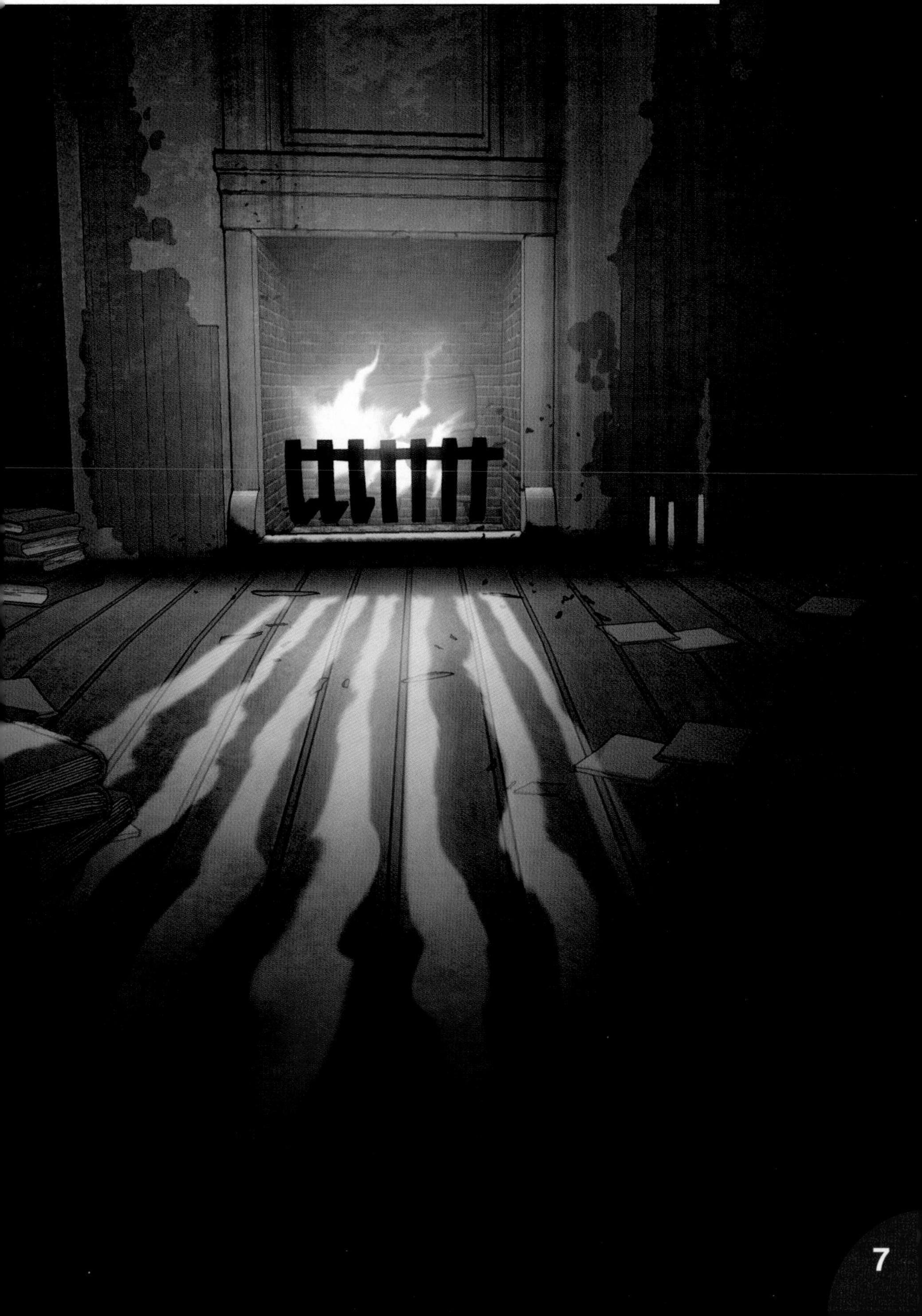

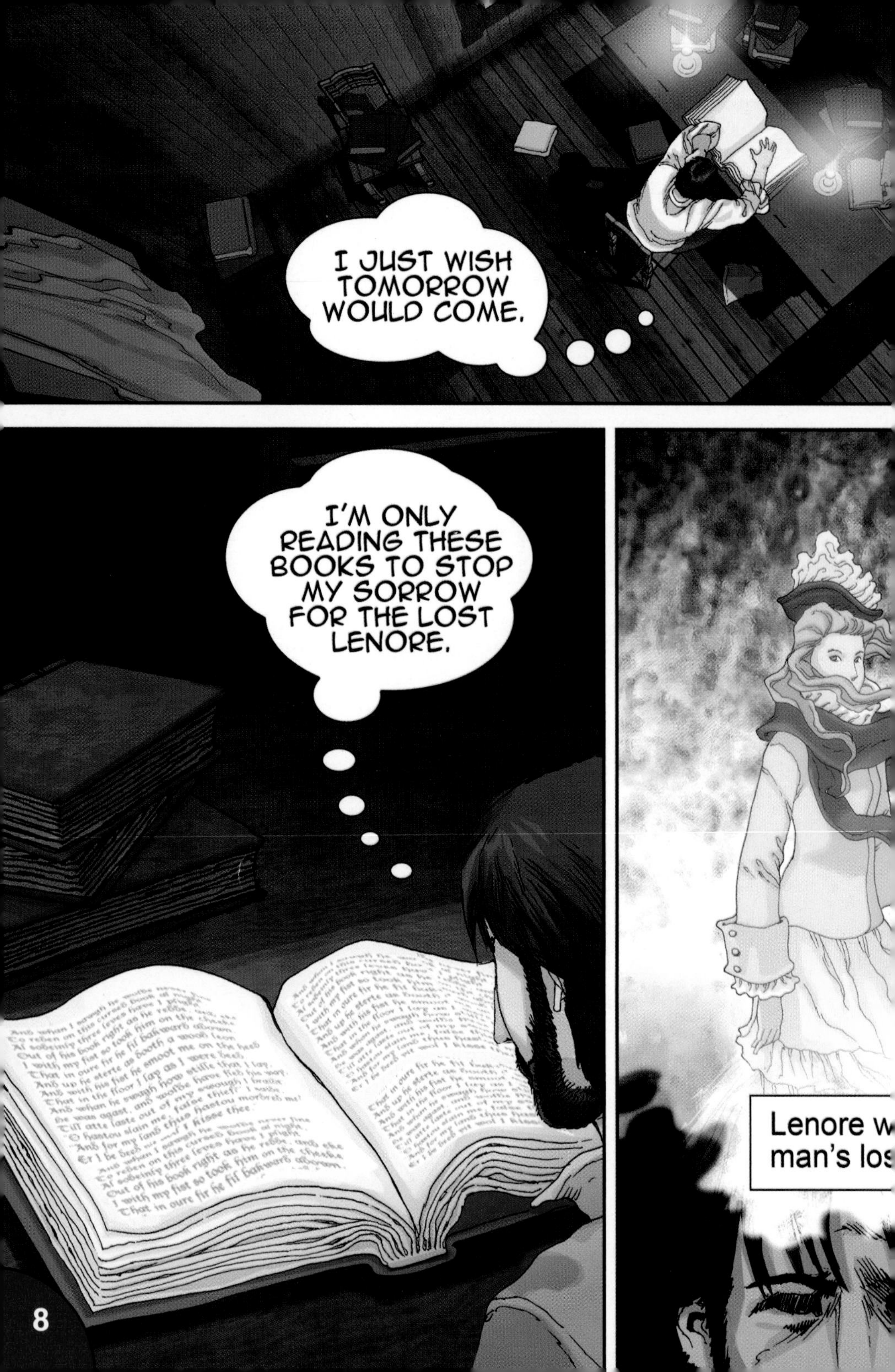
I JUST WISH TOMORROW WOULD COME.
I'M ONLY READING THESE BOOKS TO STOP MY SORROW FOR THE LOST LENORE.
Lenore w
man's los

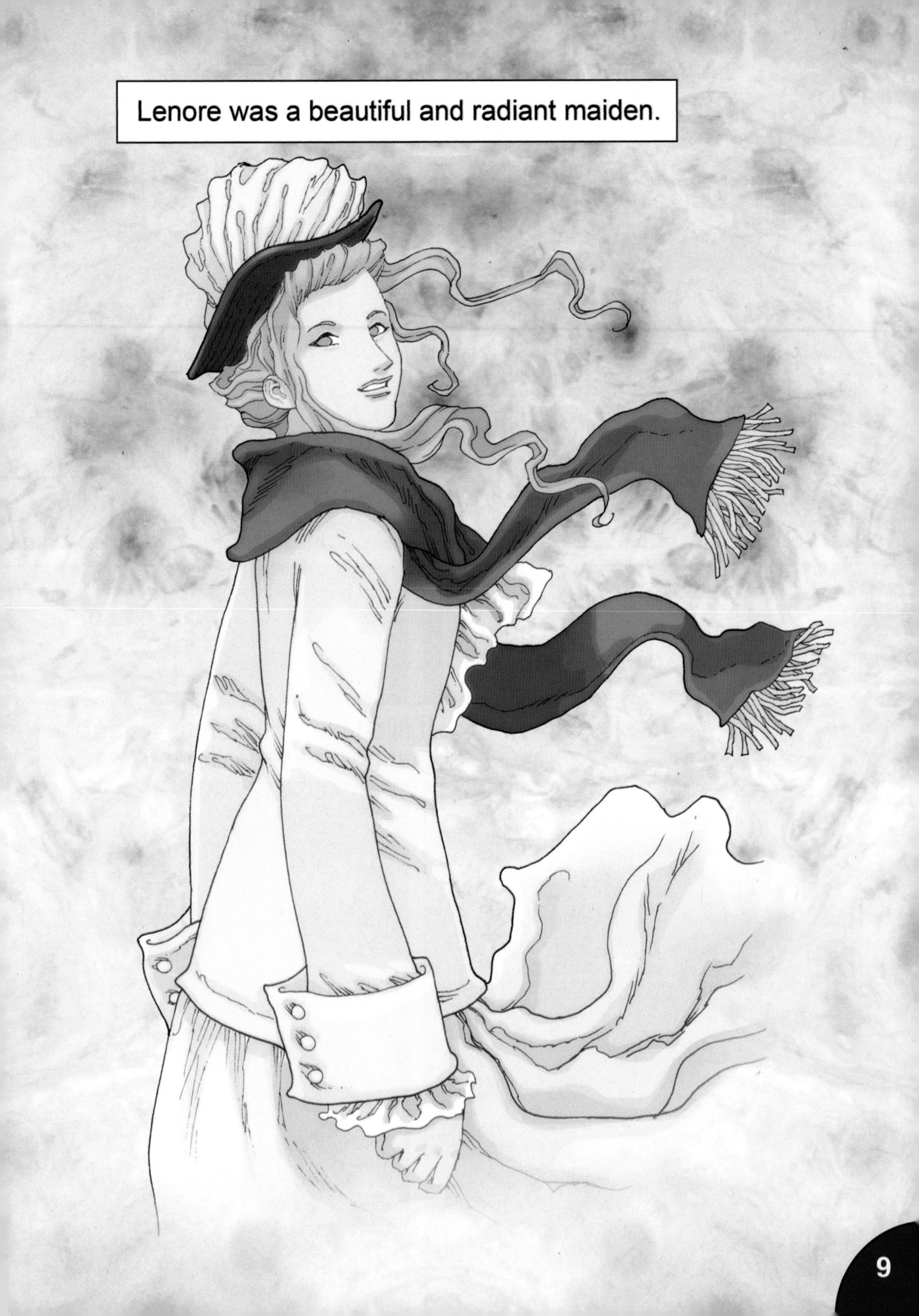
Lenore was a beautiful and radiant maiden.

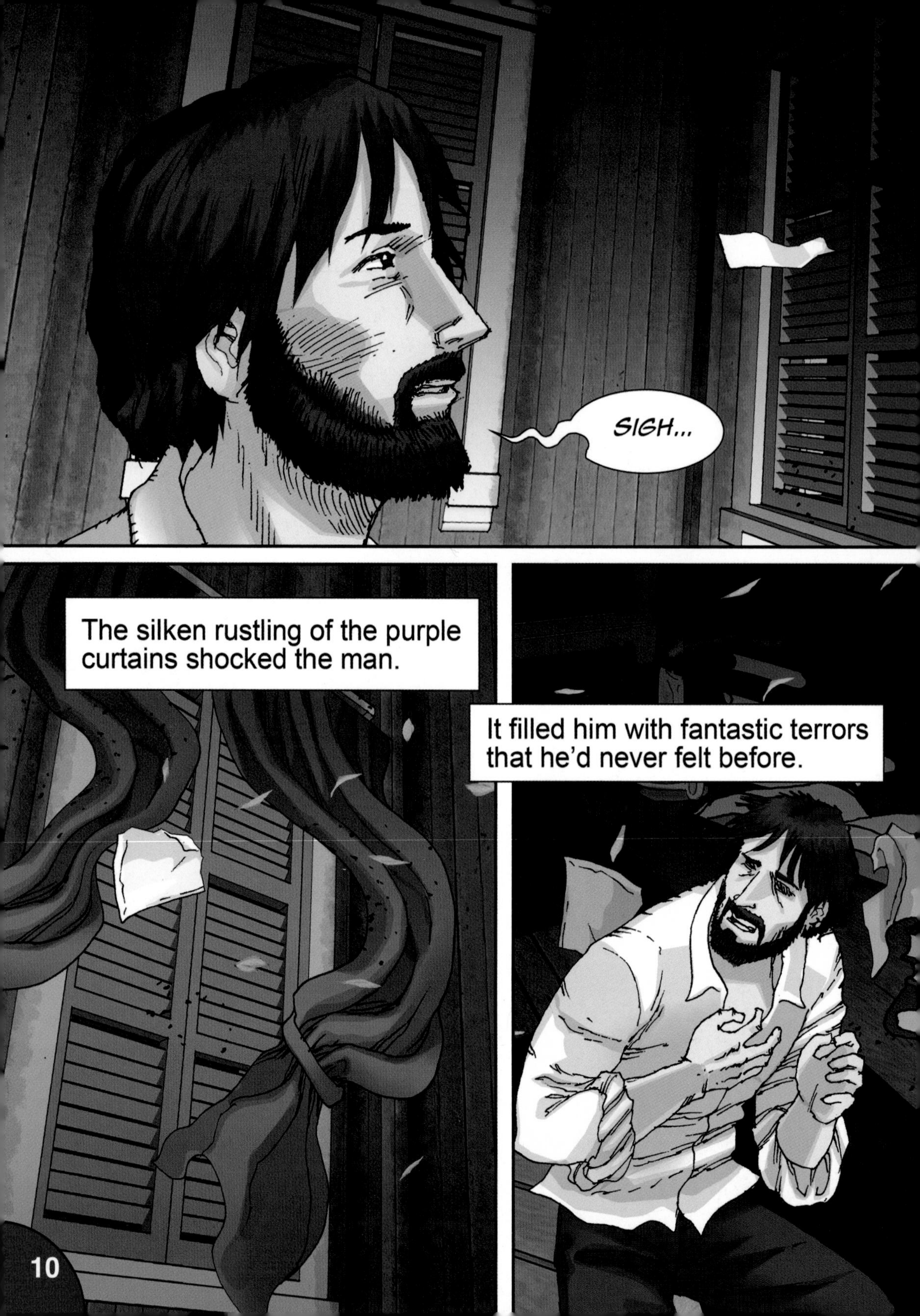
SIGH...
The silken rustling of the purple curtains shocked the man.
It filled him with fantastic terrors that he'd never felt before.

IT'S JUST A VISITOR TRYING TO ENTER MY DOOR. IT'S JUST A VISITOR TRYING TO ENTER MY DOOR. IT ISN'T ANYTHING SPOOKY.

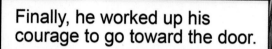

Finally, he worked up his courage to go toward the door.

SIR OR MADAM, I ASK YOUR FORGIVENESS, BUT I WAS NAPPING WHEN YOU BEGAN TAPPING AT MY DOOR. I WASN'T SURE I HEARD YOU.

He opened the door, but nothing was there.

He stood there, wondering and fearing, doubting and dreaming about what was out there.

LENORE?

All was silent except the hall echoing back t[...] man's words.

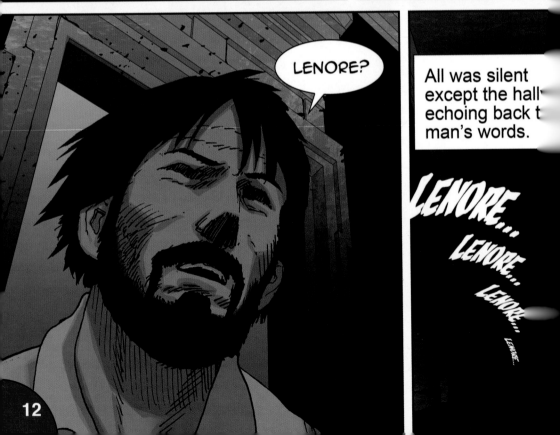

LENORE...
LENORE...
LENORE...
LENORE...

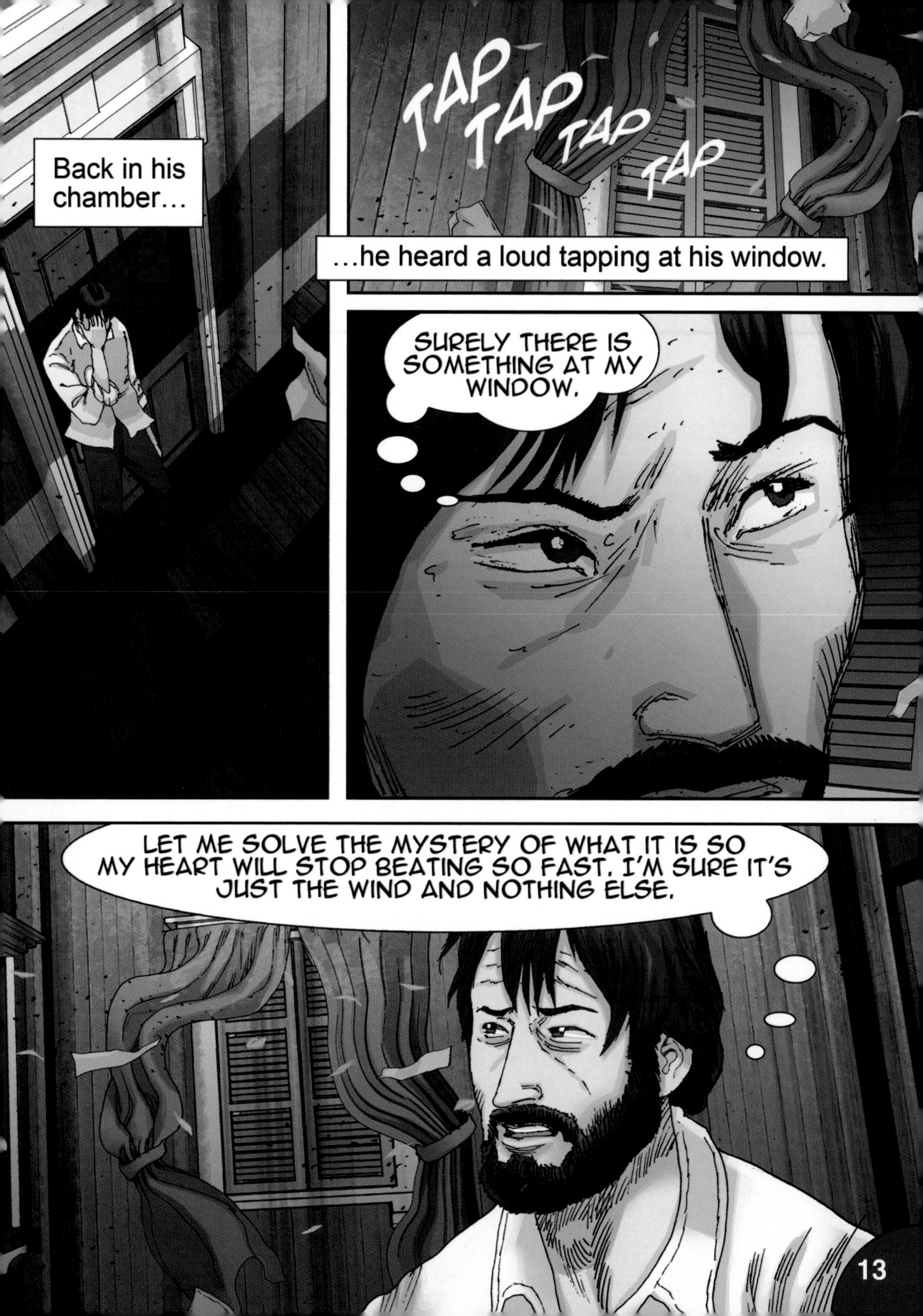
Back in his chamber…
TAP TAP TAP TAP
…he heard a loud tapping at his window.
SURELY THERE IS SOMETHING AT MY WINDOW.
LET ME SOLVE THE MYSTERY OF WHAT IT IS SO MY HEART WILL STOP BEATING SO FAST. I'M SURE IT'S JUST THE WIND AND NOTHING ELSE.

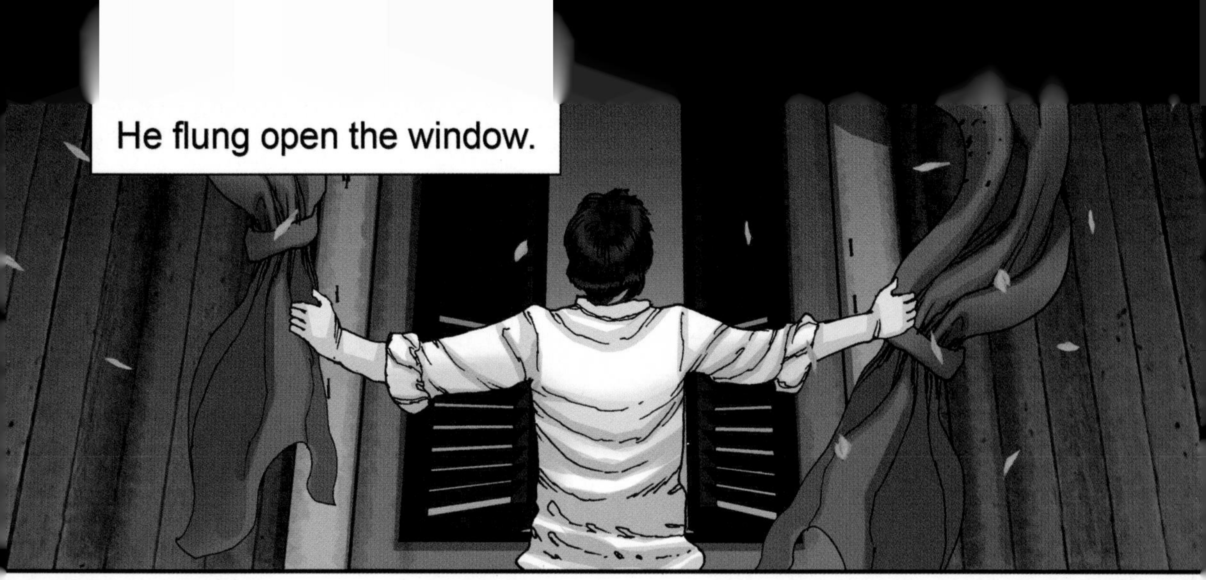
He flung open the window.

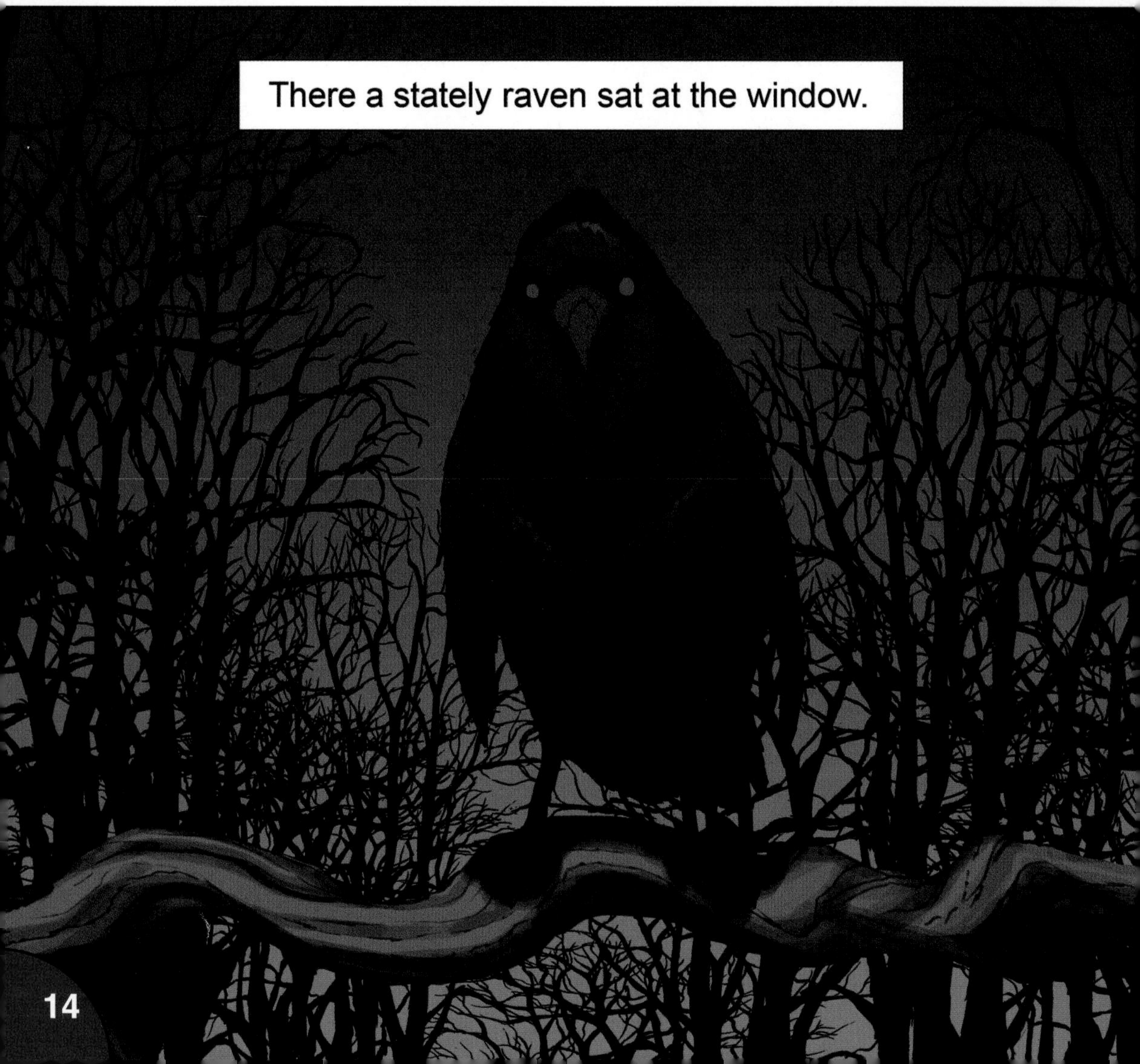
There a stately raven sat at the window.

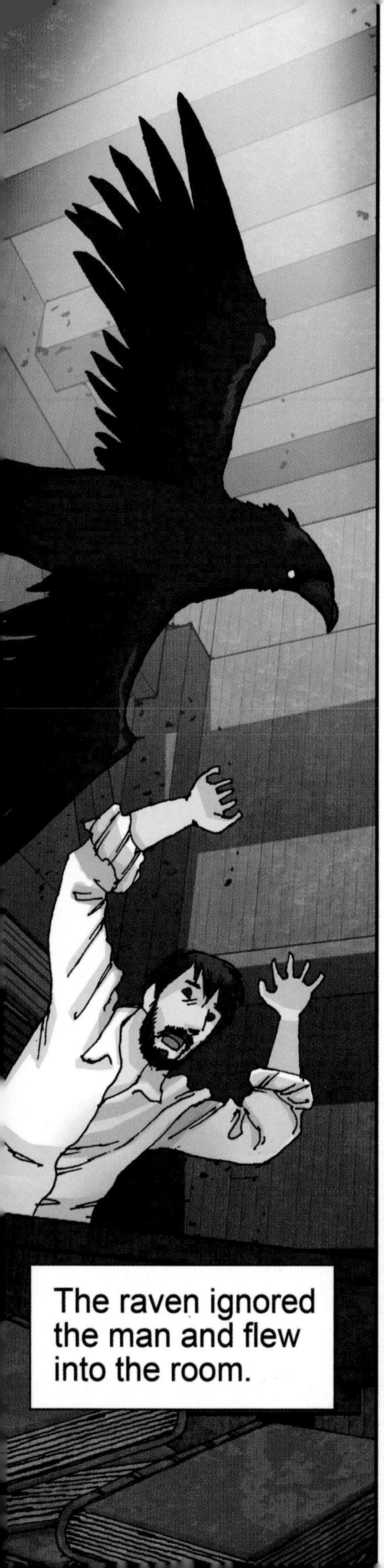
The raven ignored the man and flew into the room.
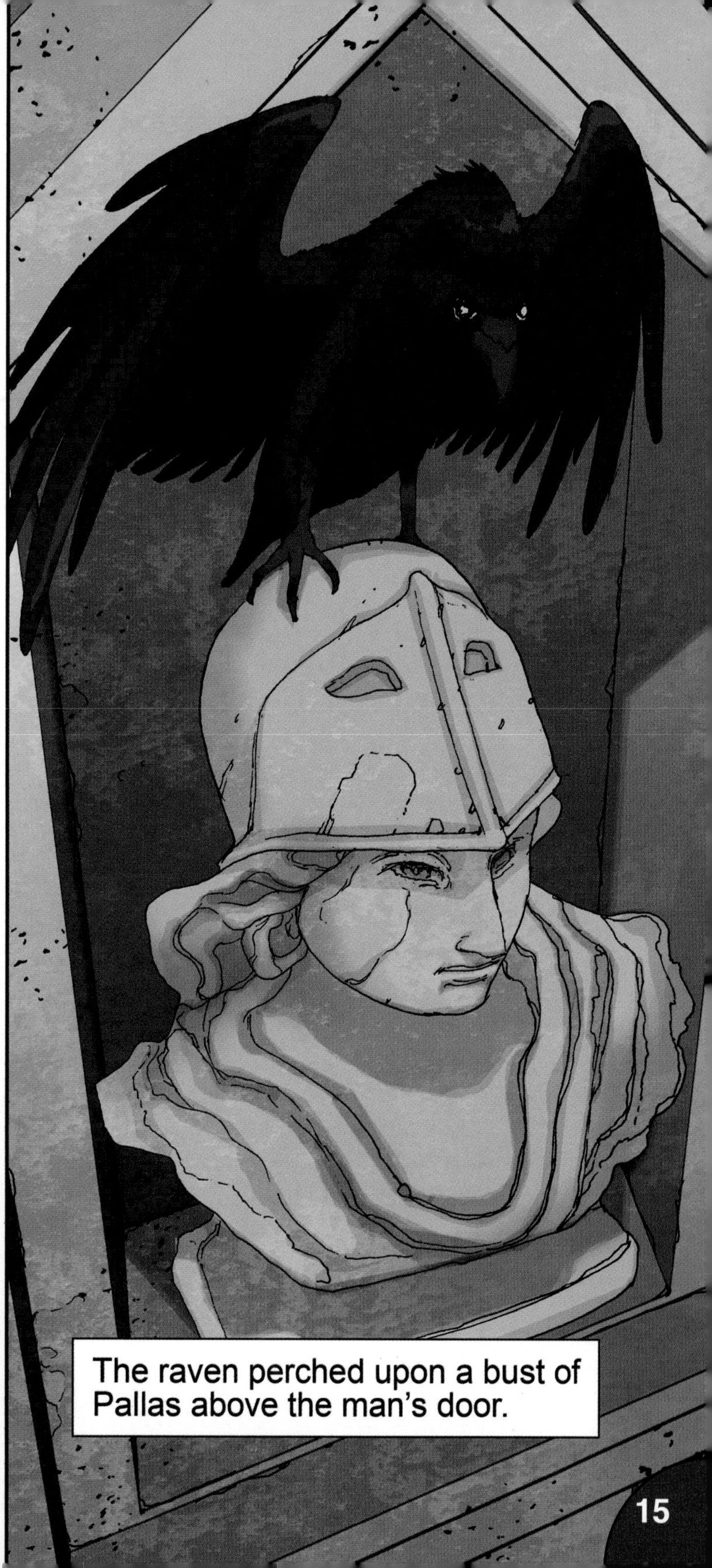
The raven perched upon a bust of Pallas above the man's door.

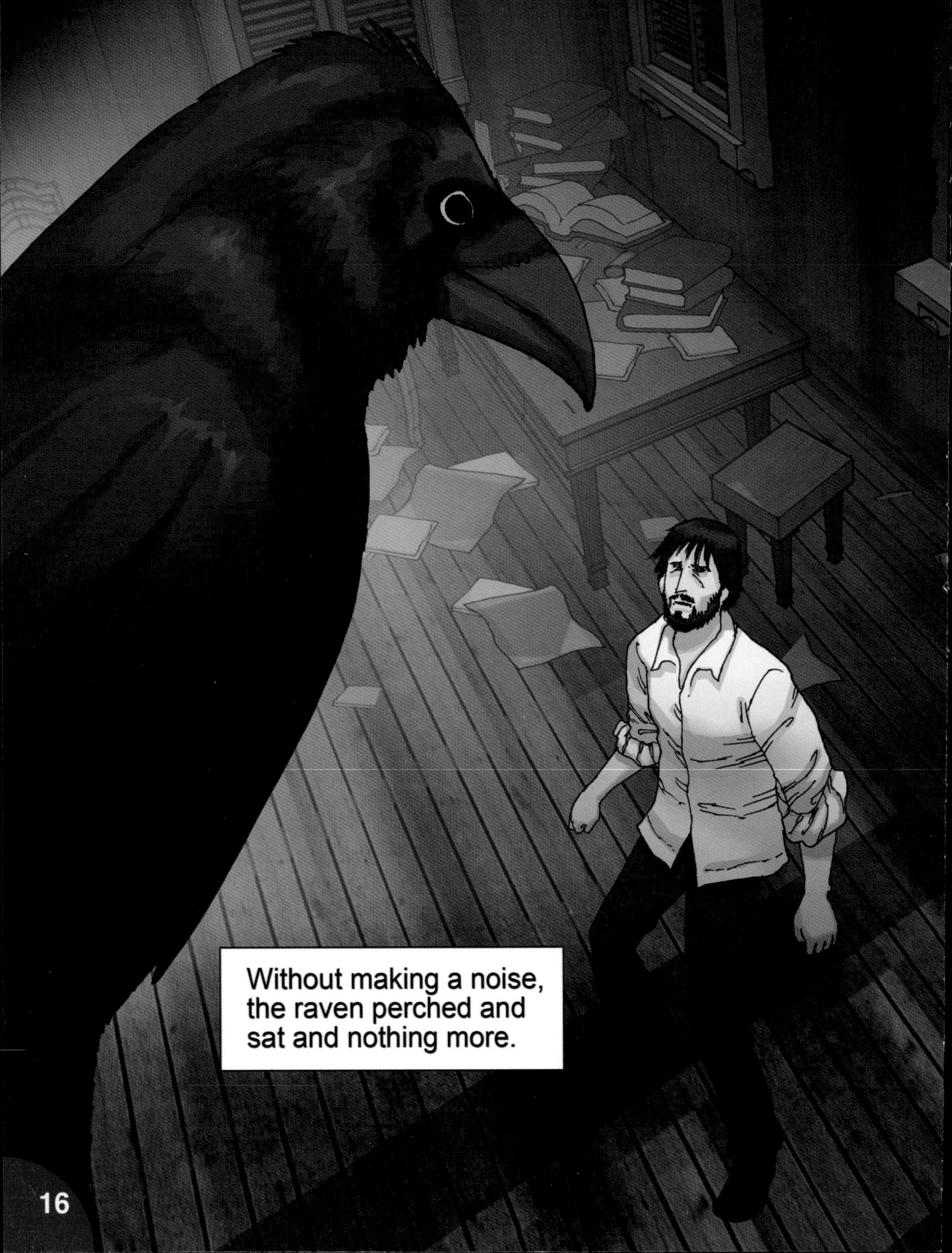
Without making a noise, the raven perched and sat and nothing more.

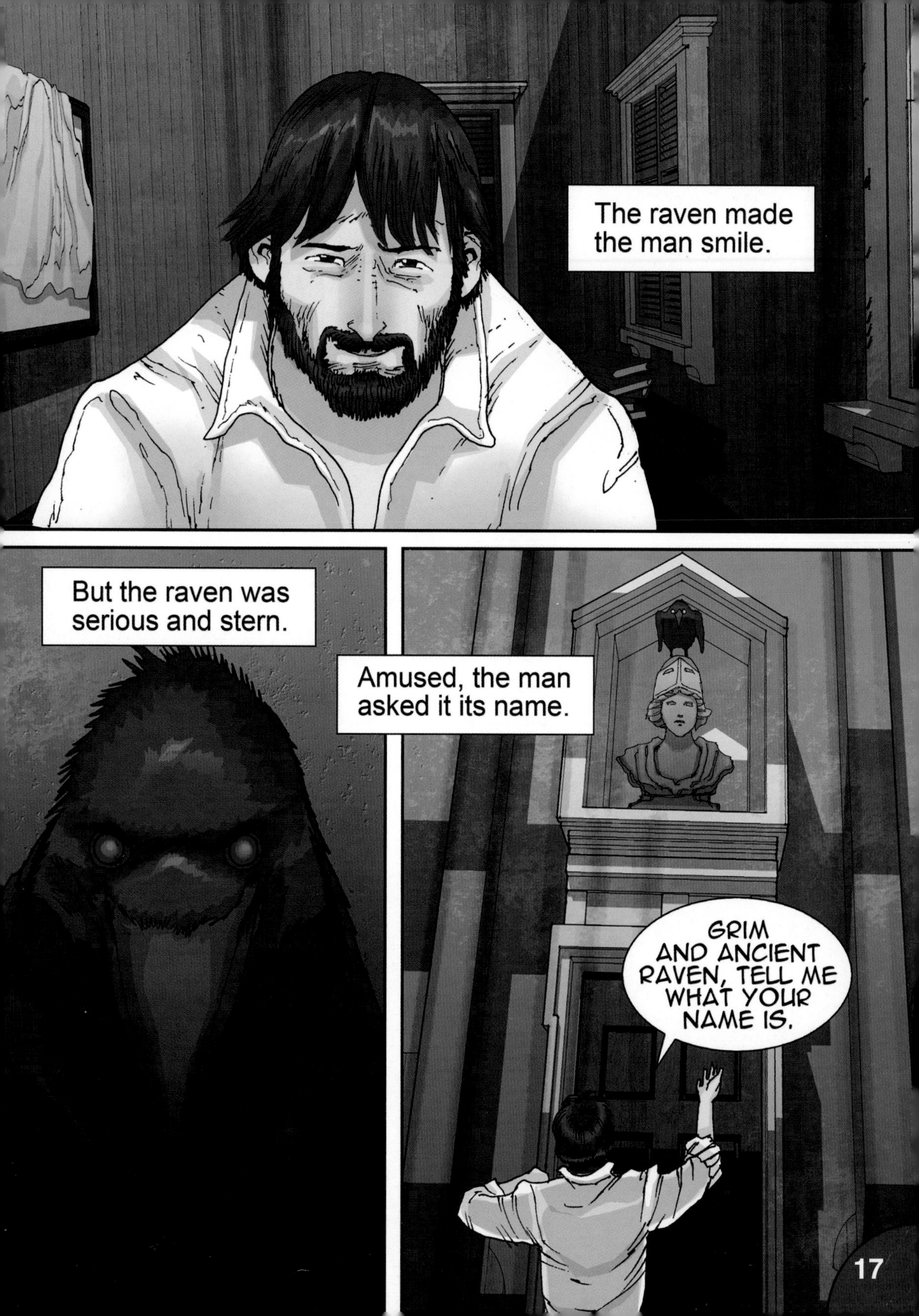
The raven made the man smile.
But the raven was serious and stern.
Amused, the man asked it its name.
GRIM AND ANCIENT RAVEN, TELL ME WHAT YOUR NAME IS.

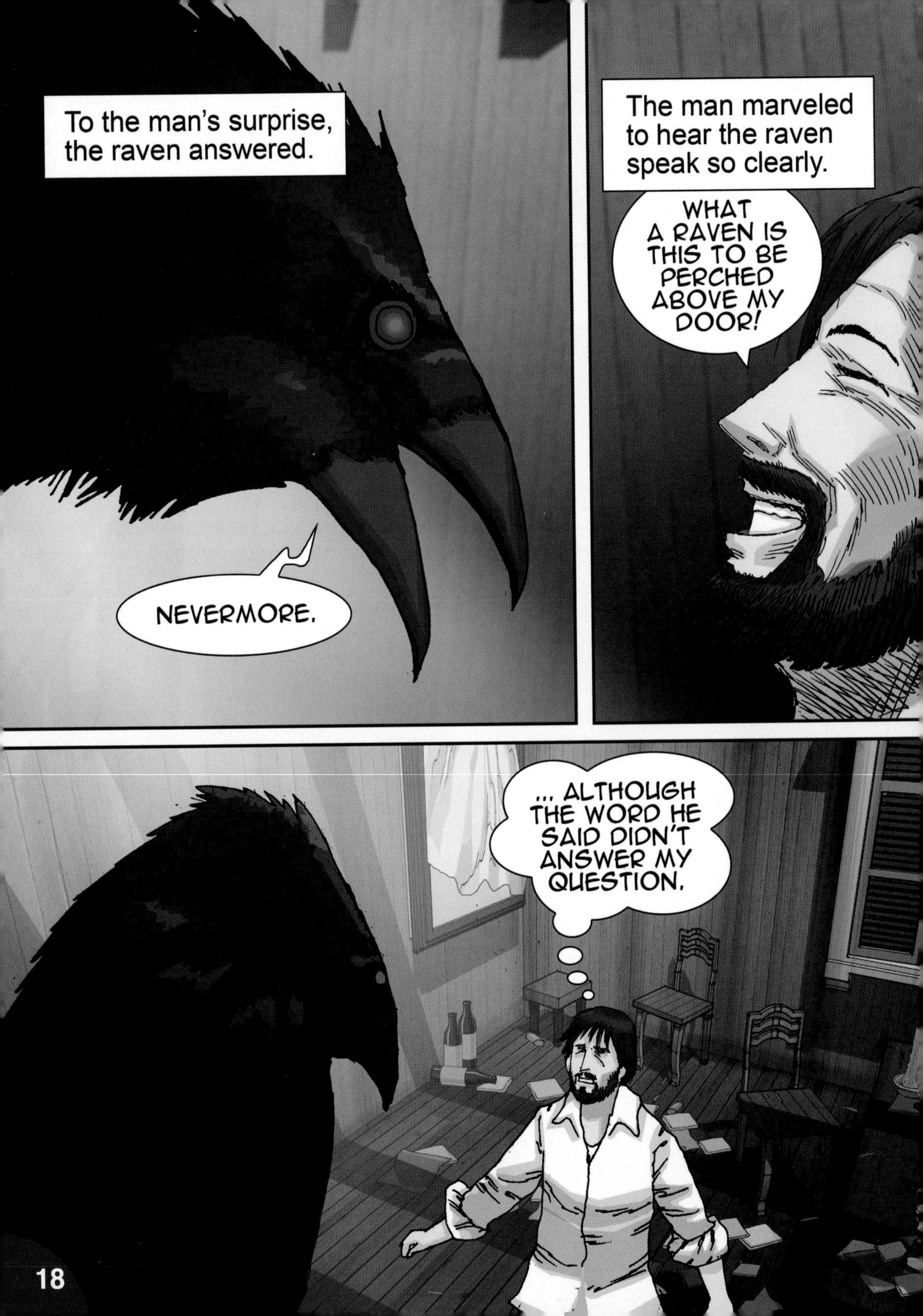
To the man's surprise, the raven answered.
NEVERMORE.
The man marveled to hear the raven speak so clearly.
WHAT A RAVEN IS THIS TO BE PERCHED ABOVE MY DOOR!
... ALTHOUGH THE WORD HE SAID DIDN'T ANSWER MY QUESTION.

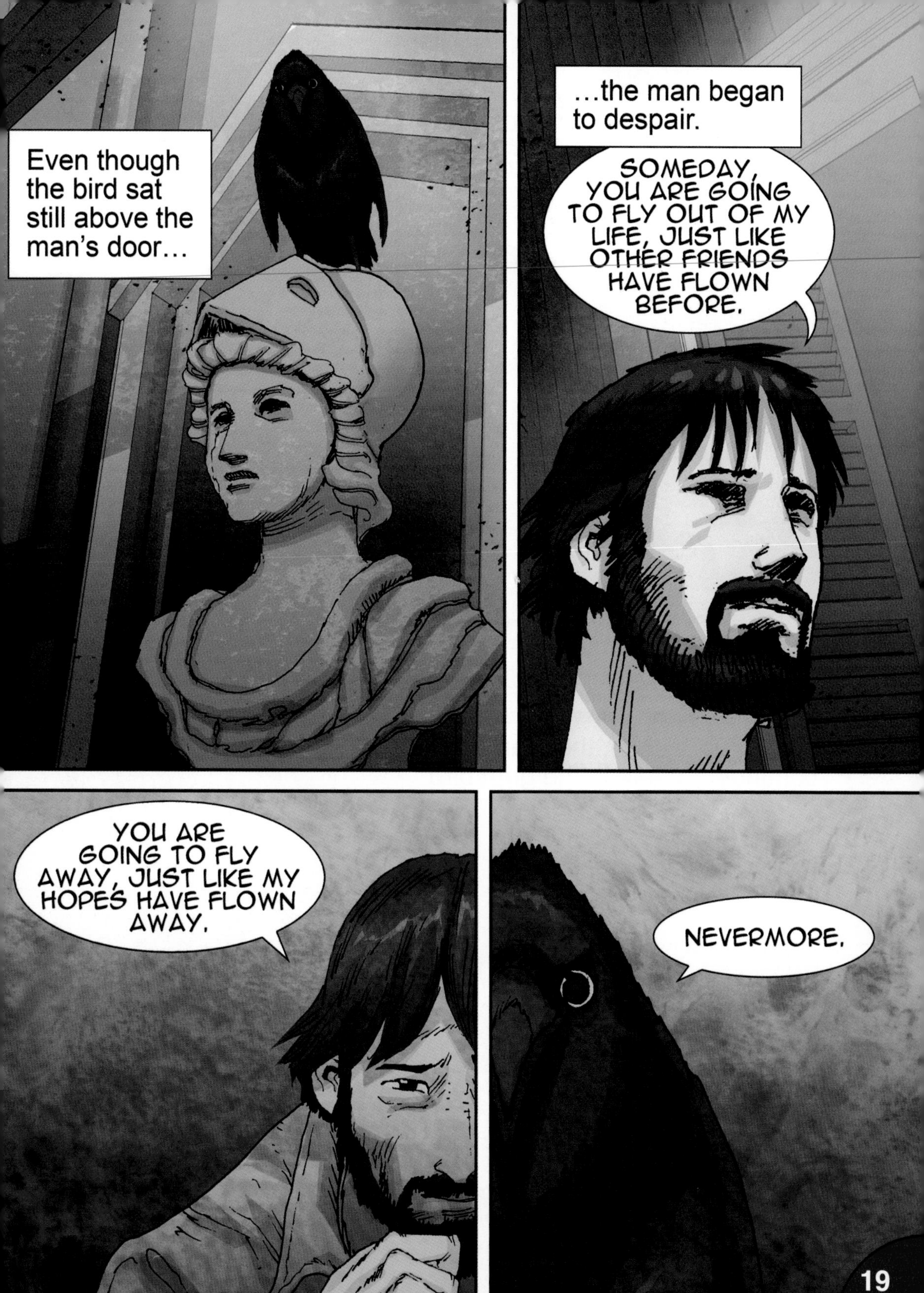
Even though the bird sat still above the man's door…
…the man began to despair.
SOMEDAY, YOU ARE GOING TO FLY OUT OF MY LIFE, JUST LIKE OTHER FRIENDS HAVE FLOWN BEFORE.
YOU ARE GOING TO FLY AWAY, JUST LIKE MY HOPES HAVE FLOWN AWAY.
NEVERMORE.

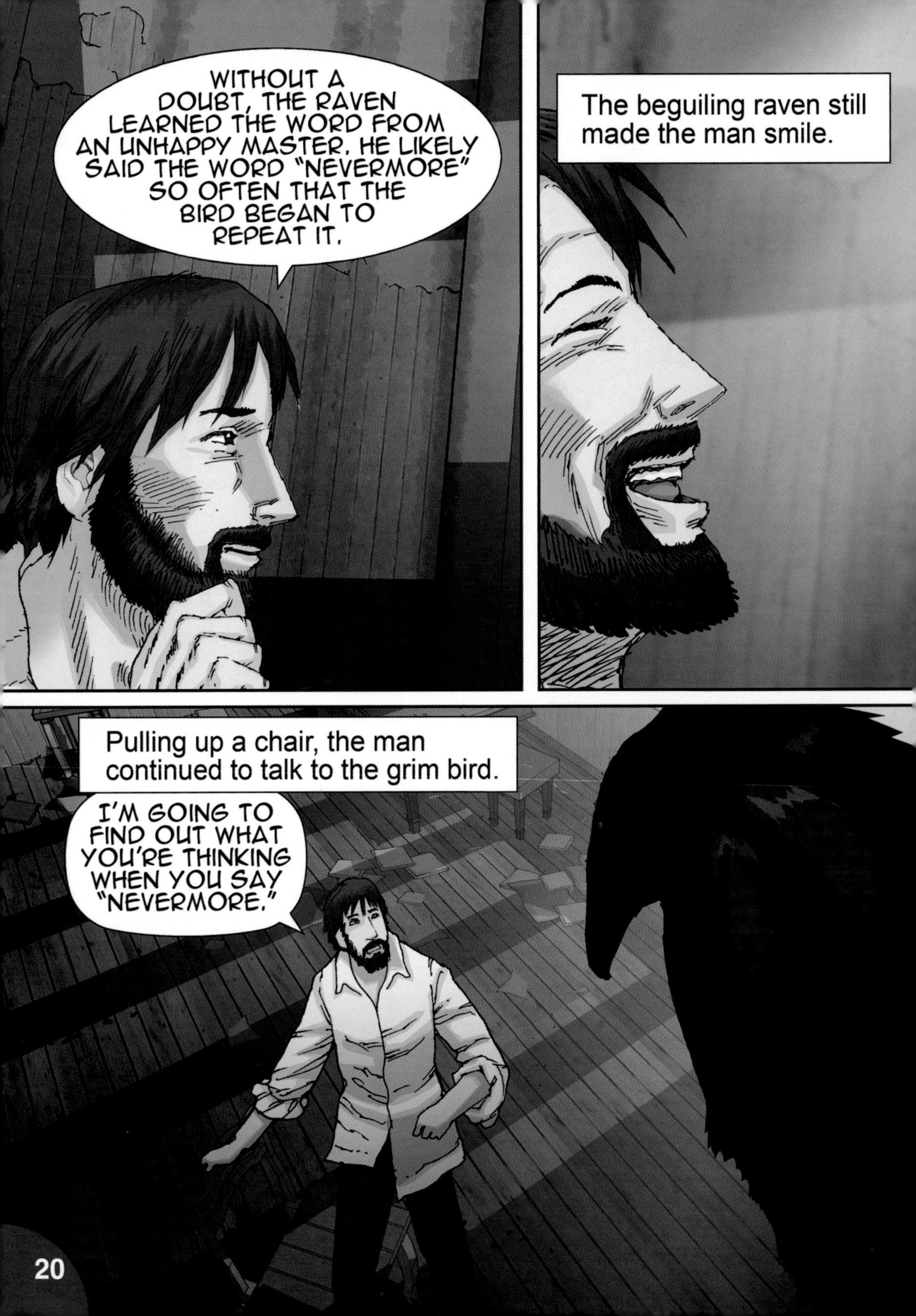
WITHOUT A DOUBT, THE RAVEN LEARNED THE WORD FROM AN UNHAPPY MASTER. HE LIKELY SAID THE WORD "NEVERMORE" SO OFTEN THAT THE BIRD BEGAN TO REPEAT IT.
The beguiling raven still made the man smile.
Pulling up a chair, the man continued to talk to the grim bird.
I'M GOING TO FIND OUT WHAT YOU'RE THINKING WHEN YOU SAY "NEVERMORE."

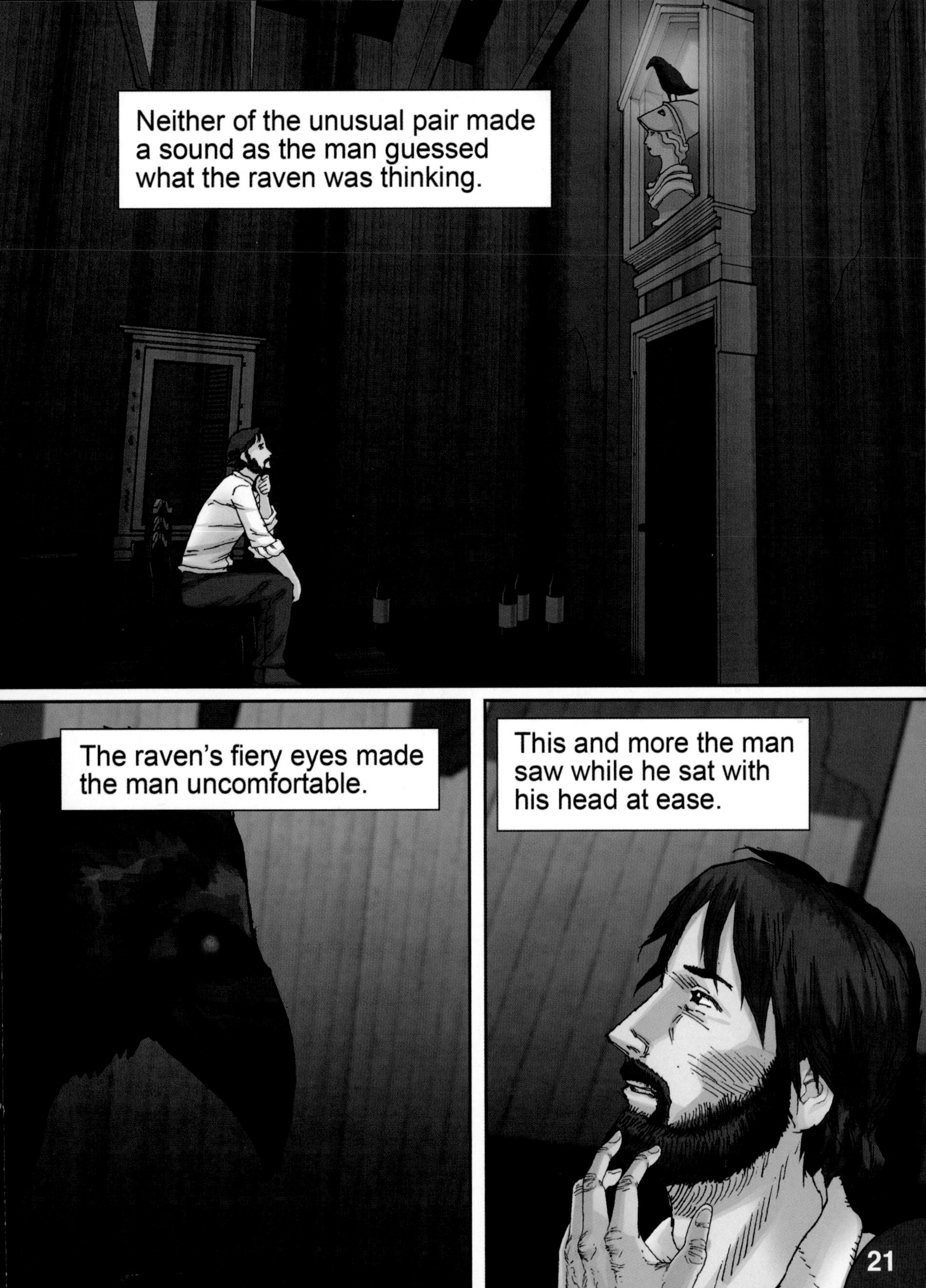
Neither of the unusual pair made a sound as the man guessed what the raven was thinking.
The raven's fiery eyes made the man uncomfortable.
This and more the man saw while he sat with his head at ease.

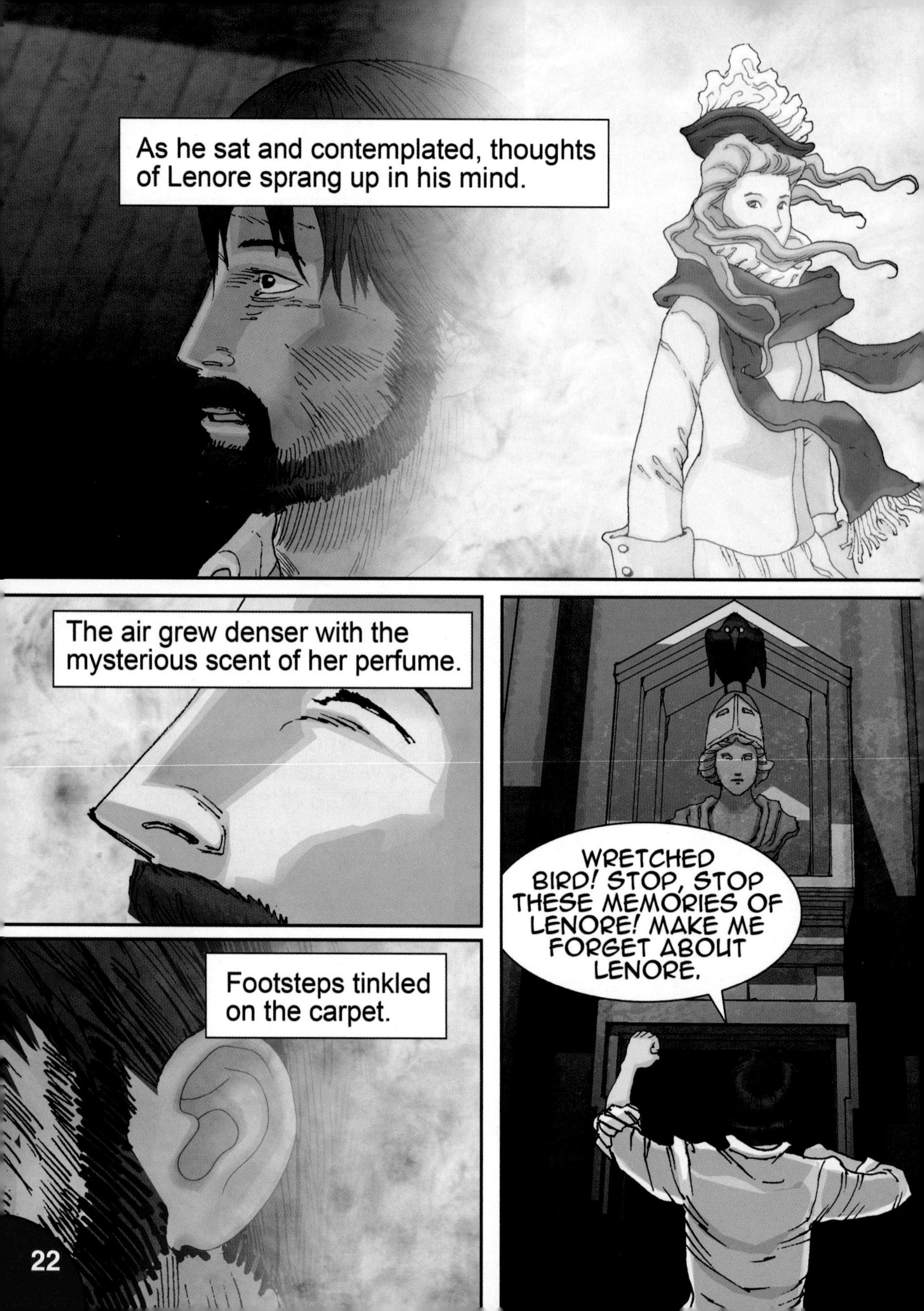
As he sat and contemplated, thoughts of Lenore sprang up in his mind.
The air grew denser with the mysterious scent of her perfume.
Footsteps tinkled on the carpet.
WRETCHED BIRD! STOP, STOP THESE MEMORIES OF LENORE! MAKE ME FORGET ABOUT LENORE.

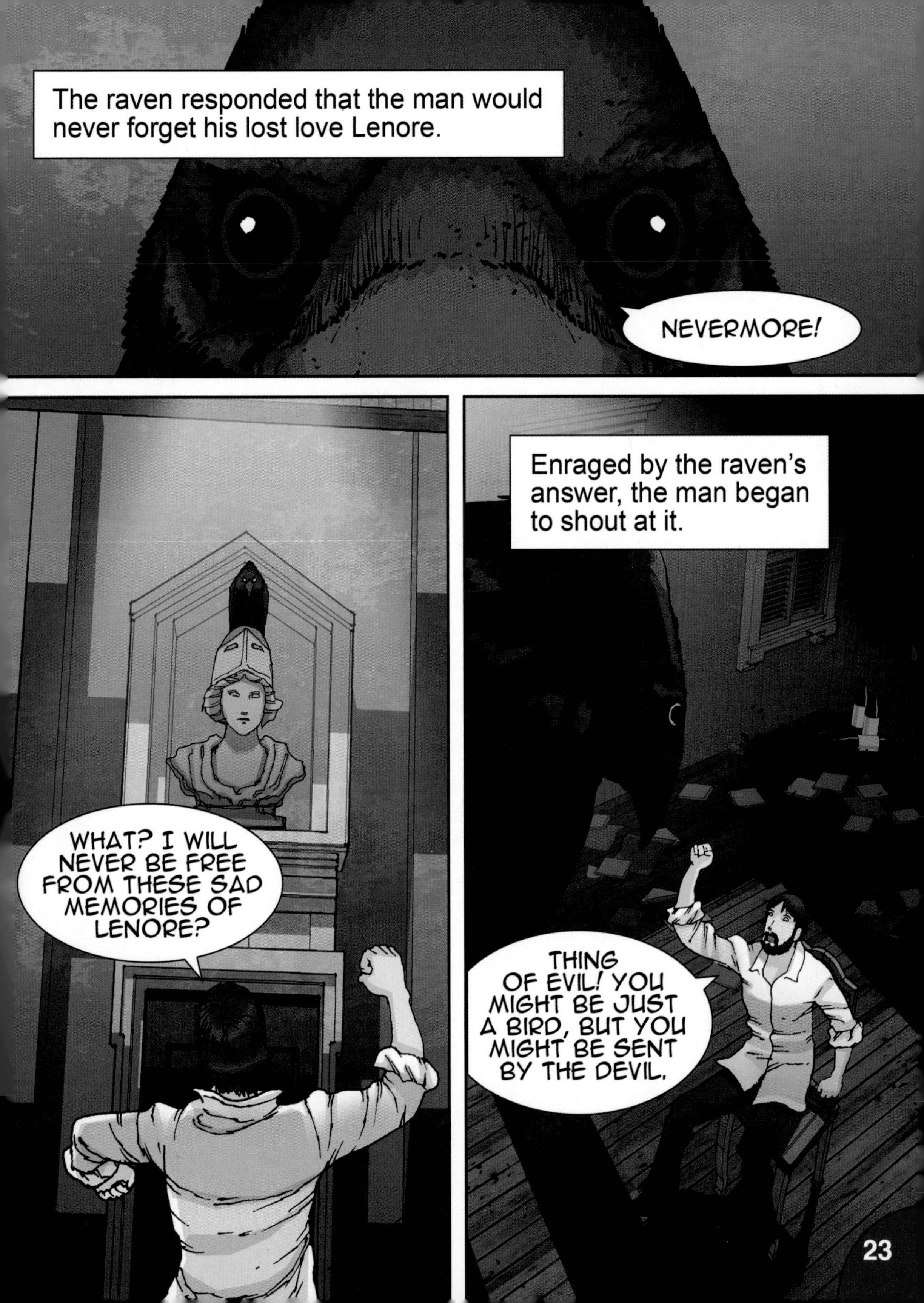
The raven responded that the man would never forget his lost love Lenore.
NEVERMORE!
WHAT? I WILL NEVER BE FREE FROM THESE SAD MEMORIES OF LENORE?
Enraged by the raven's answer, the man began to shout at it.
THING OF EVIL! YOU MIGHT BE JUST A BIRD, BUT YOU MIGHT BE SENT BY THE DEVIL.

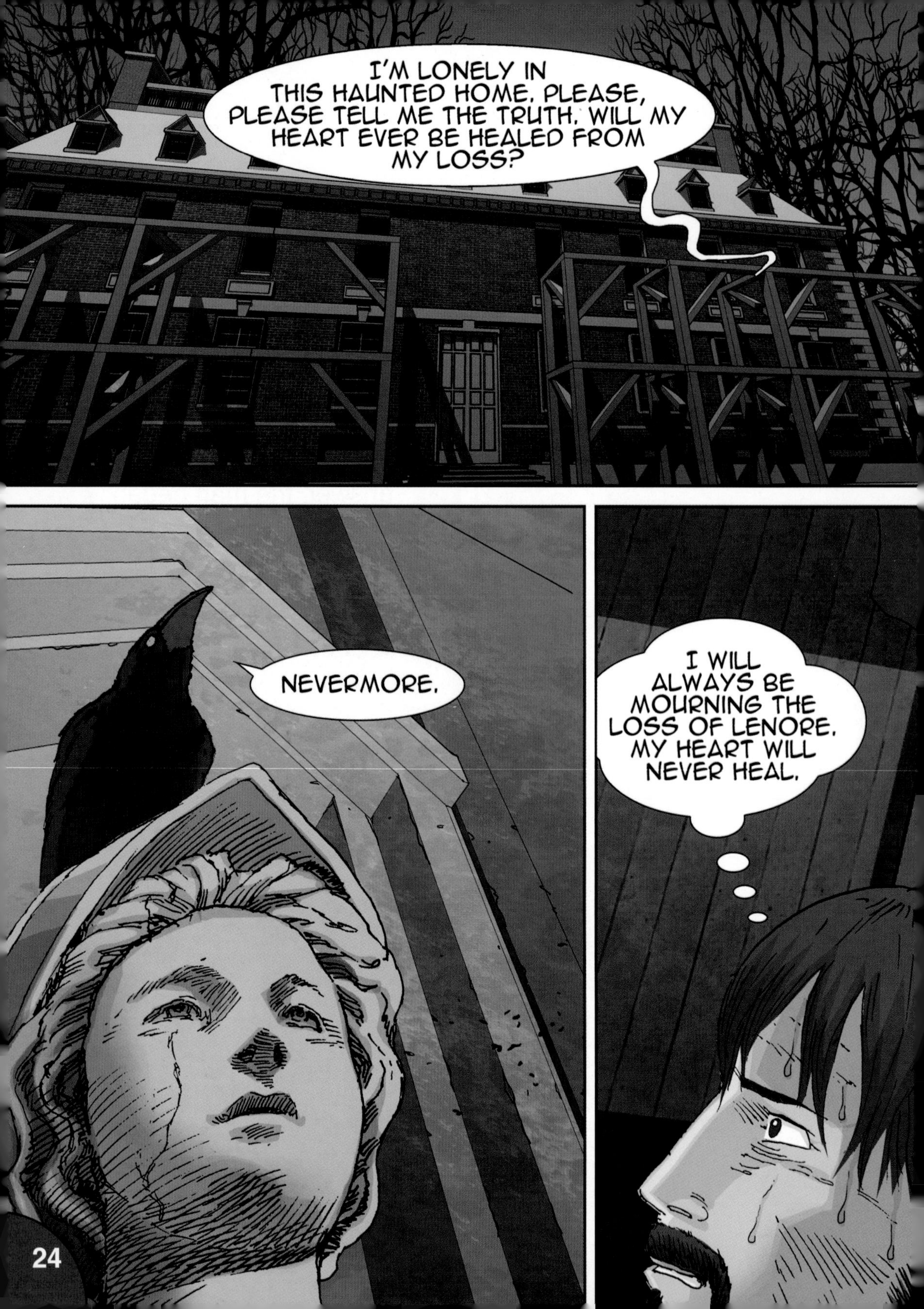
I'M LONELY IN THIS HAUNTED HOME. PLEASE, PLEASE TELL ME THE TRUTH. WILL MY HEART EVER BE HEALED FROM MY LOSS?
NEVERMORE.
I WILL ALWAYS BE MOURNING THE LOSS OF LENORE. MY HEART WILL NEVER HEAL.

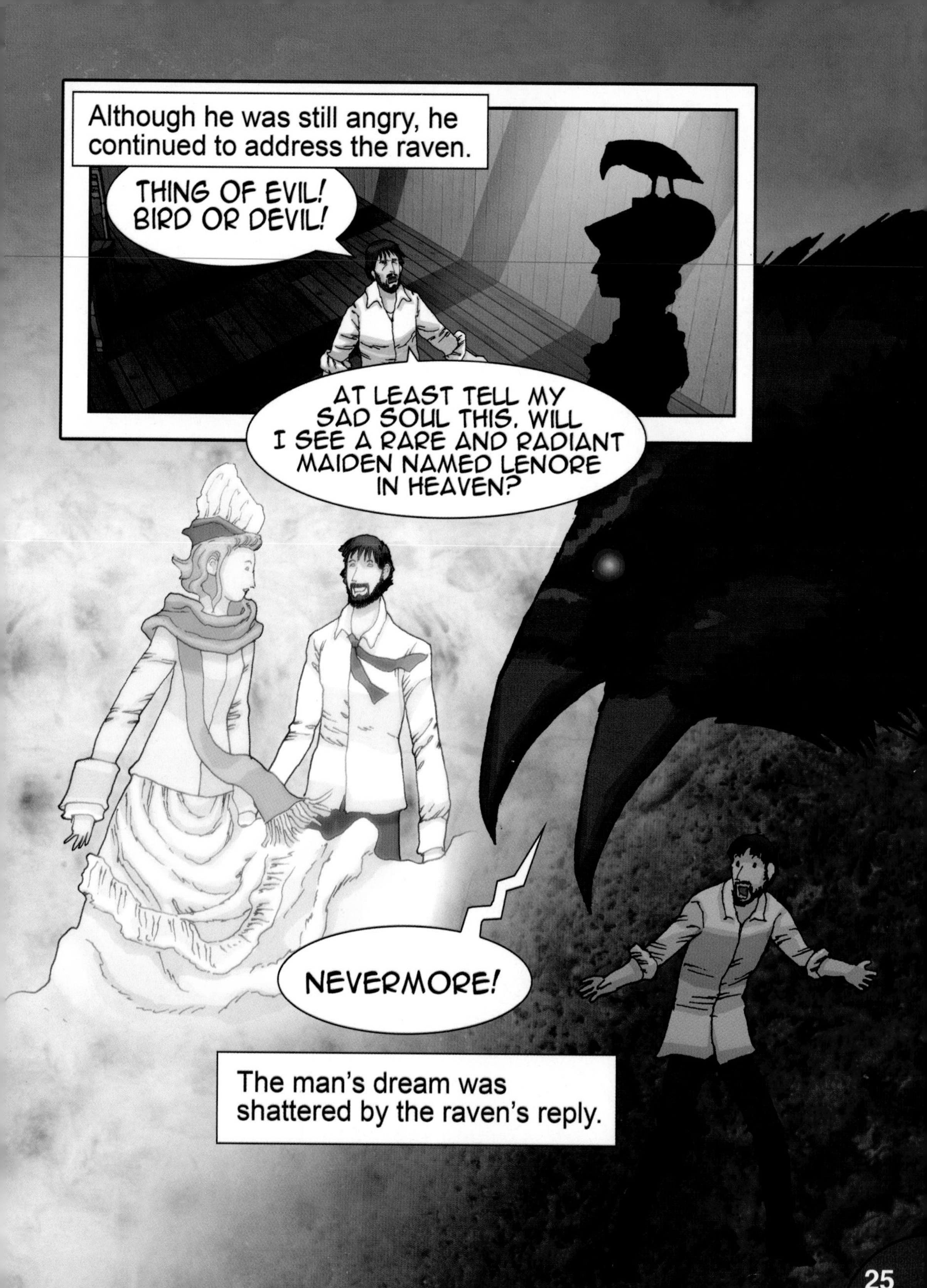
Although he was still angry, he continued to address the raven.
THING OF EVIL! BIRD OR DEVIL!
AT LEAST TELL MY SAD SOUL THIS. WILL I SEE A RARE AND RADIANT MAIDEN NAMED LENORE IN HEAVEN?
NEVERMORE!
The man's dream was shattered by the raven's reply.

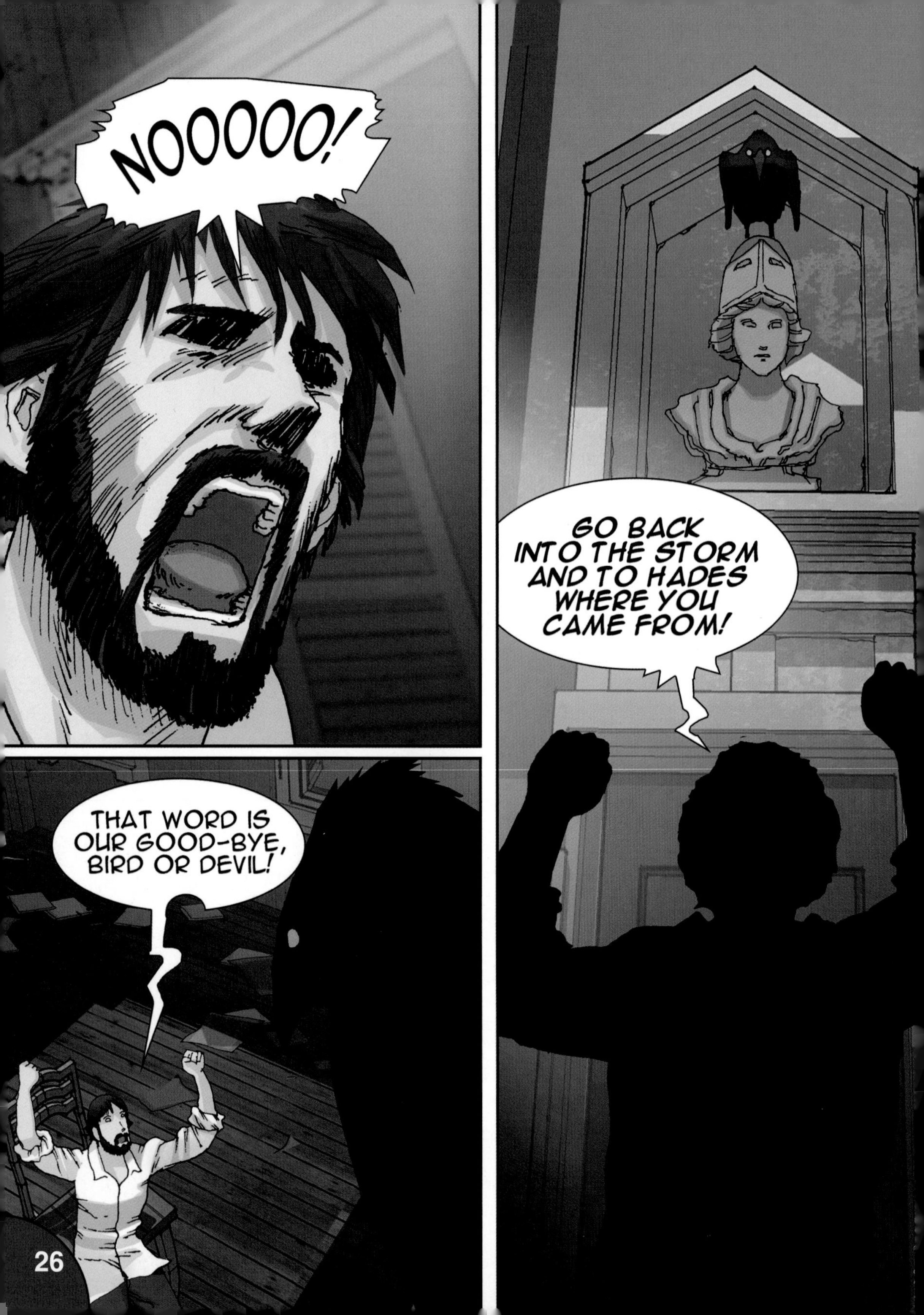
NOOOOO!
GO BACK INTO THE STORM AND TO HADES WHERE YOU CAME FROM!
THAT WORD IS OUR GOOD-BYE, BIRD OR DEVIL!

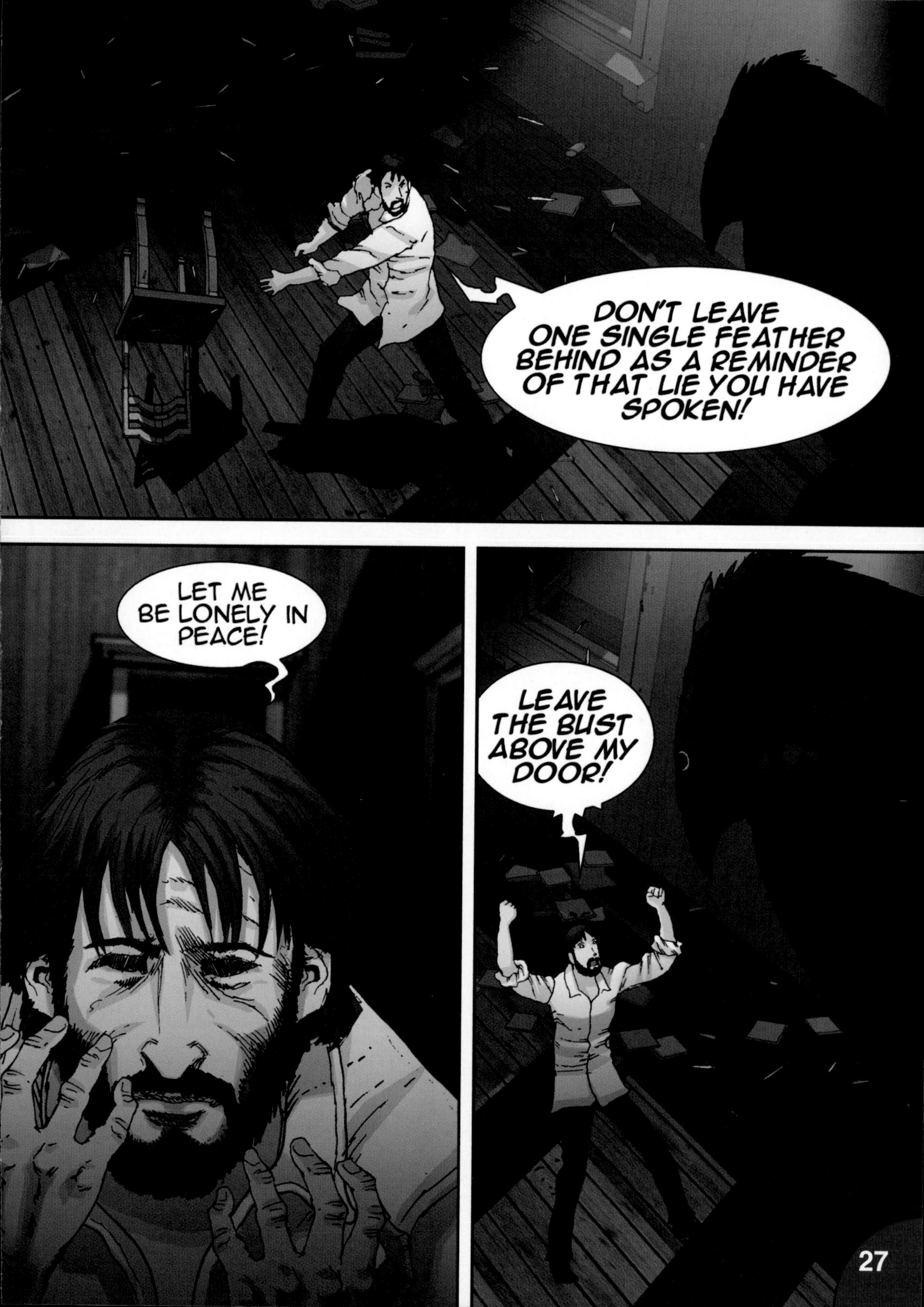
DON'T LEAVE ONE SINGLE FEATHER BEHIND AS A REMINDER OF THAT LIE YOU HAVE SPOKEN!
LET ME BE LONELY IN PEACE!
LEAVE THE BUST ABOVE MY DOOR!

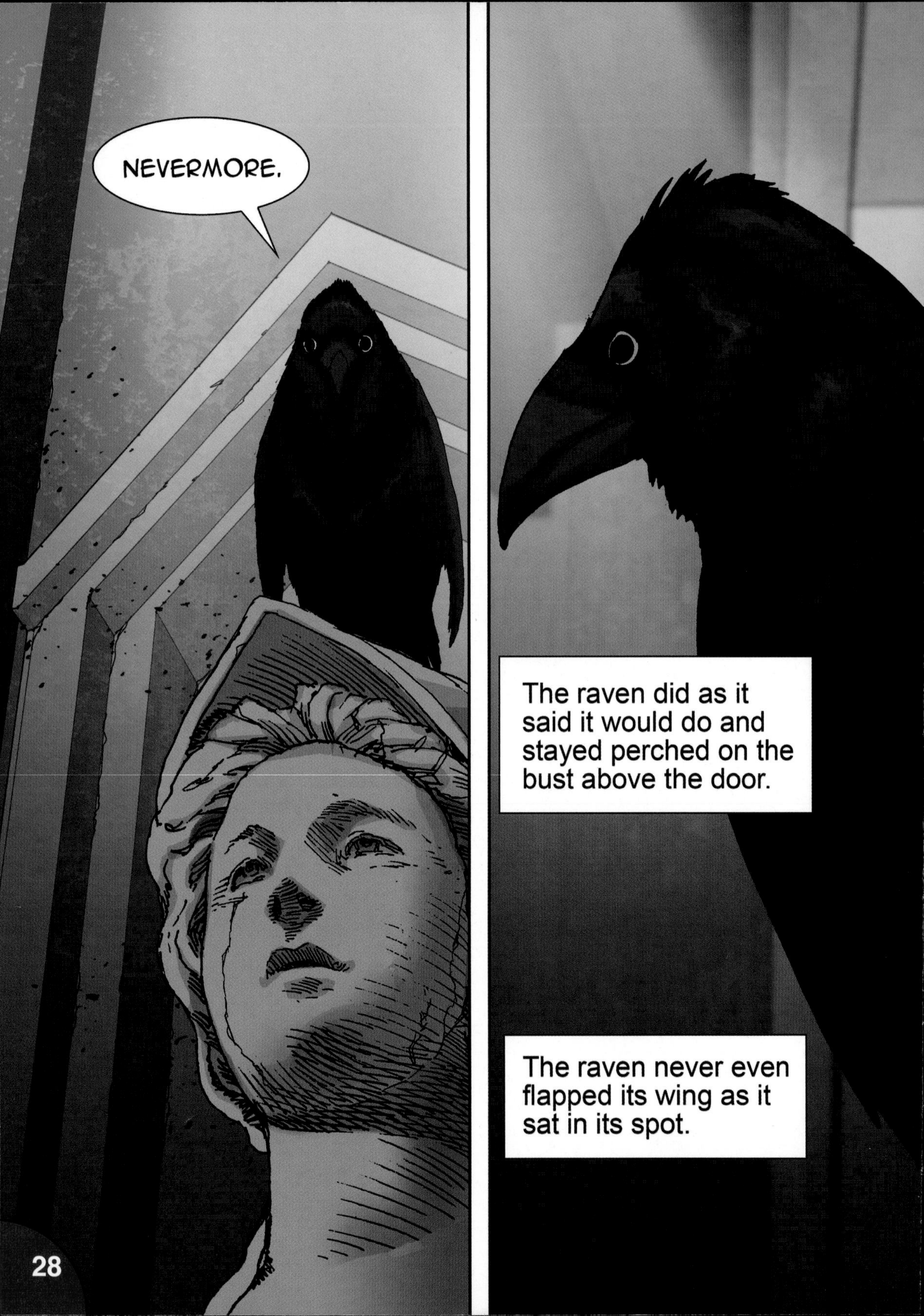
NEVERMORE.
The raven did as it said it would do and stayed perched on the bust above the door.
The raven never even flapped its wing as it sat in its spot.

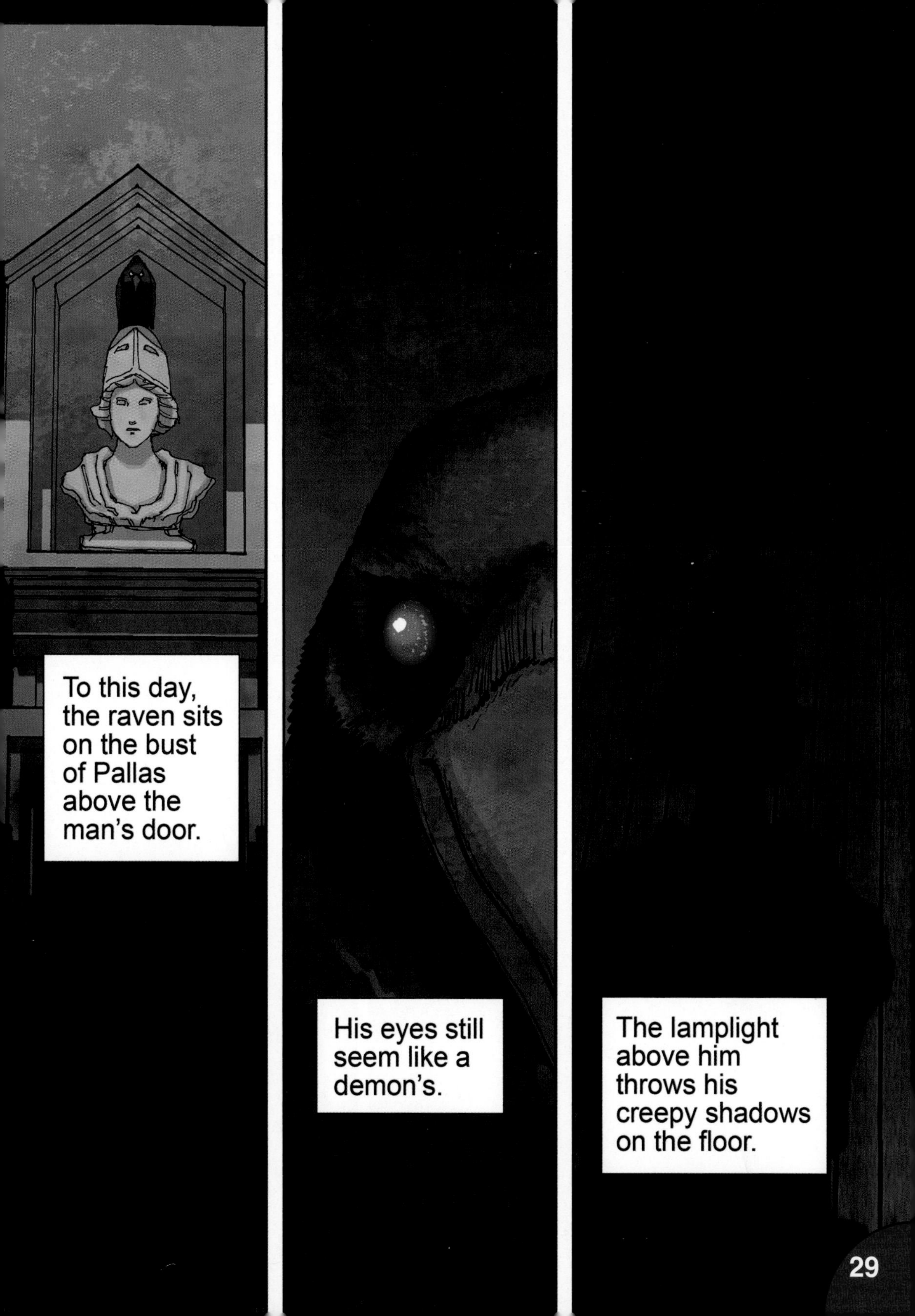
To this day, the raven sits on the bust of Pallas above the man's door.
His eyes still seem like a demon's.
The lamplight above him throws his creepy shadows on the floor.

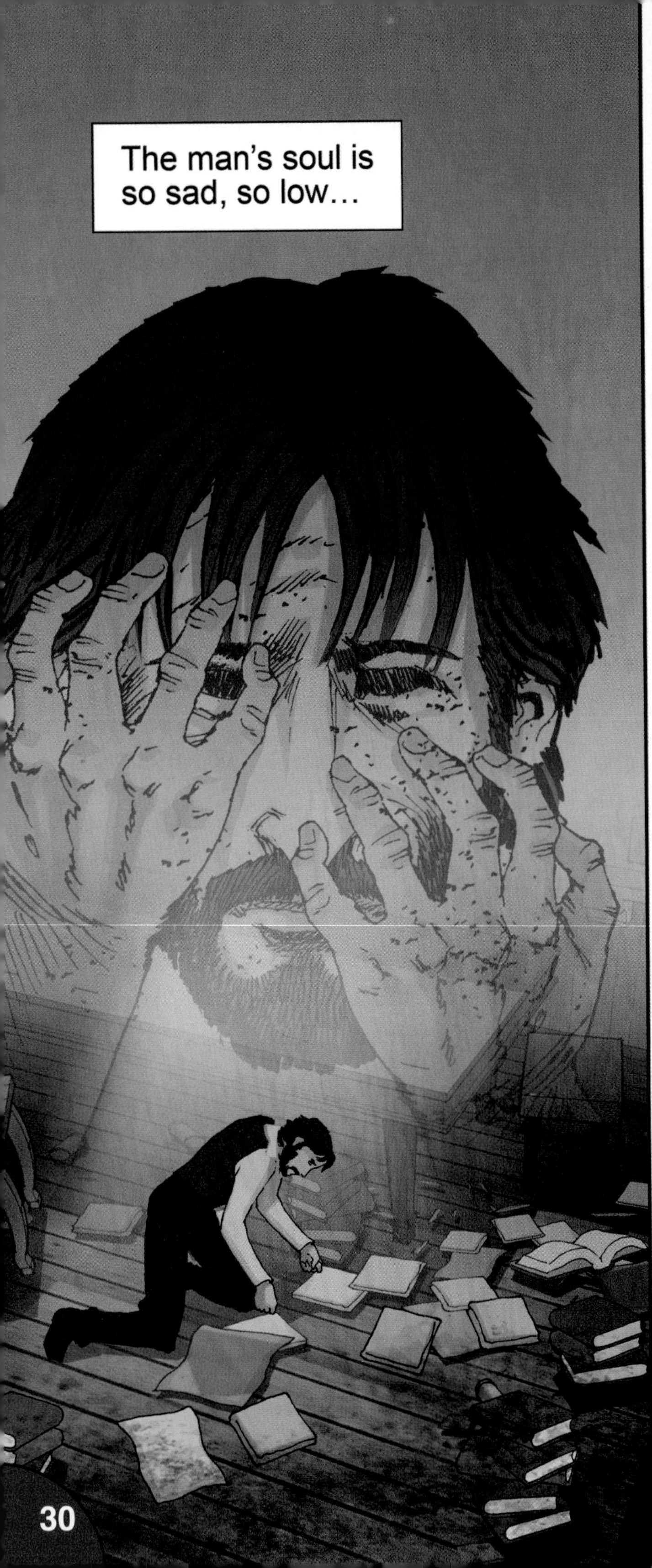
The man's soul is so sad, so low…

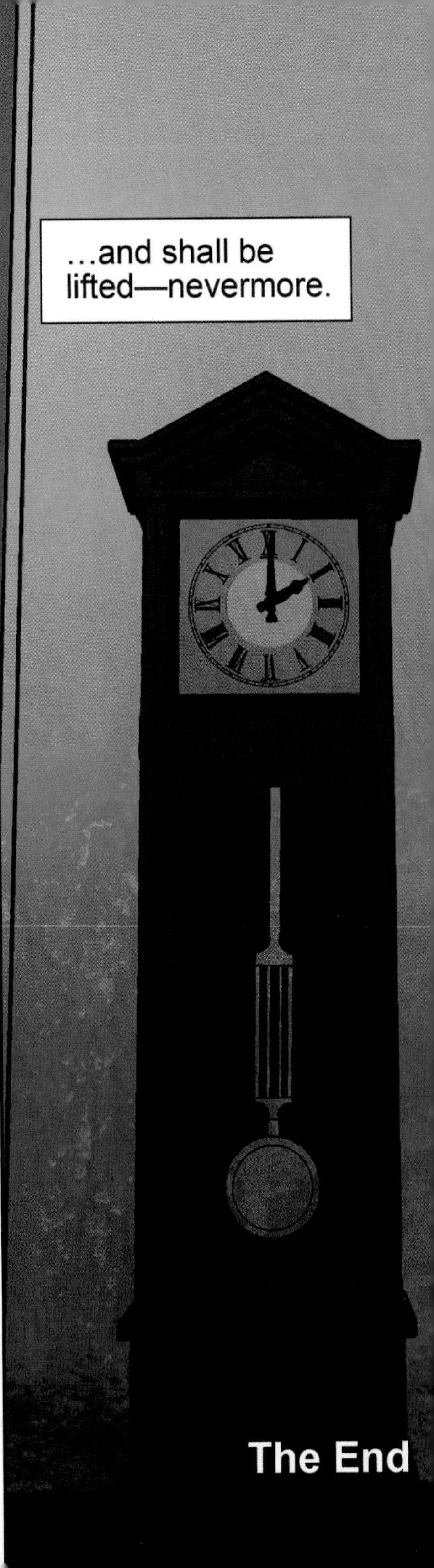
…and shall be lifted—nevermore.
The End

About the Author

Edgar Allan Poe was born on January 19, 1809, in Boston, Massachusetts. His parents, Elizabeth Arnold Poe and David Poe Jr., were both actors. After his mother died in 1811, Edgar lived with his godfather John Allan in Richmond, Virginia. He was later sent to England and Scotland for schooling. In 1826, he attended the University of Virginia for 11 months.

In 1827, Poe published a pamphlet of poems. He then joined the army under the name Edgar A. Perry. Two years later, Allan purchased Poe's release from the army and got him into the U.S. Military Academy at West Point. Poe was expelled from West Point in 1831, and his education ended.

Poe continued to write poetry and eventually short stories filled with terror and sadness. He won several prizes for his writing. By 1835, Poe had become an editor at a magazine in Richmond. The next year, he married his young cousin Virginia Clemm.

Early on, Poe made a name for himself as a critical reviewer. He held several different editing jobs throughout his life. But, it wasn't until his poem "The Raven" was published in 1845 that he became famous.

Poe died on October 7, 1849, in Baltimore, Maryland. Today, Edgar Allan Poe is often remembered for his tales of mystery and death. He remains an important influence on many writers.

Additional Works

The Fall of the House of Usher (1839)
The Gold Bug (1843)
The Tell-Tale Heart (1843)
The Raven (1845)
The Cask of Amontillado (1846)
Eureka (1848)
Annabel Lee (1849)

Glossary

beguiling - to trick someone by being cunning.

bust - a sculpture of a person's head and shoulders.

contemplate - to consider with a lot of attention for a period of time.

despair - having no hope.

Hades - the Greek name for the underworld.

radiant - glowing with love, confidence, or happiness.

stately - impressively grand in size, manner, or appearance.

wretched - evil.

3 1333 04219 0817

Web Sites

To learn more about Edgar Allan Poe, visit the ABDO Group online at **www.abdopublishing.com**. Web sites about Poe are featured on our Book Links page. These links are routinely monitored and updated to provide the most current information available.